To DADDY & MOTHER —
For so many HAPPY HOLIDAYS!
AND FOR HABITAT FOR HUMANITY
— A LITTLE PRE-THANKSGIVING
AND PRE-CHRISTMAS READING!
I LOVE you much,
GEE

Home for the Holidays

Home for the holidays

Stories and Art
Created for the Benefit of
Habitat for Humanity

Edited by Gene Stelten,
with a preface by Jimmy Carter
and an introduction by Millard Fuller

All proceeds received by Habitat for
Humanity from the sale of this book will
be used to build low-cost housing with
families in need. On behalf of the
hundreds of families on our waiting lists,
thank you in advance for purchasing
this book.

PEACHTREE
ATLANTA

℗
PUBLISHED BY
Peachtree Publishers, Ltd.
494 Armour Circle NE
Atlanta, Georgia 30324

Excerpt from *The Book of Virtues*, © 1993 by William J. Bennett. Simon & Schuster, New York. Used by permission.
Excerpt from *Family—The Ties That Bind—And Gag!*, © 1987 by Erma Bombeck. McGraw-Hill, New York. Used by permission.
Excerpt from *Loving Each Other*, © 1984 by Leo Buscaglia, Inc., Slack Inc., Thorofare, New Jersey. Used by permission.
Excerpt from *Barbara Bush: A Memoir*, © 1994 by Barbara Bush. A Lisa Drew Book, Charles Scribner's Sons, New York. Used by permission.
Excerpt from "Address to the National Prayer Breakfast Luncheon," by Hillary Rodham Clinton, February 2, 1994. Used by permission.
Excerpt from *The Diary of Mario M. Cuomo: The Campaign for Governor* © 1994 by Mario M. Cuomo. Random House, New York. Used by permission.
Excerpt from "Amy Grant: Another New Beginning," by Jim Long. *Campus Life* magazine, July/August 1994. Christianity Today, Inc., Carol Stream, Illinois. Used by permission.
Excerpt from "Why John Grisham Teaches Sunday School," by Will Norton, Jr., *Christianity Today* magazine, 10-3-94. Used by permission.
Excerpt from *My Life with Martin Luther King, Jr.*, © 1994 by Coretta Scott King. Puffin Books, New York. Used by permission.
Excerpt from *On the Road With Charles Kuralt*, © 1985 by CBS, Inc. G. P. Putnam's Sons, New York. Used by permission of the author.

Jacket and book design by Terri Fox.
Jacket illustration by Steve Frenkel.

All cover art and interior illustrations have been donated by the artists for the benefit of Habitat for Humanity.

Manufactured in the United States.

10 9 8 7 6 5 4 3 2 1

First printing

Library of Congress Cataloguing-in-Publication Data

Home for the holidays : a collection of stories and art for the benefit of habitat for humanity / edited by Gene Stelten.
        p. cm.
      ISBN 1-56145-114-2 (hc)
            1. Holidays—United States—Miscellanea. 2. United States—
      Social life and customs—Miscellanea. I. Stelten, Gene, 1928- .
GT4803.A2H66 1995   95-16366
394.2'6973—dc20   CIP

To all the wonderful families who will be
HOME FOR THE HOLIDAYS
in a warm Habitat house.

To Brittany and Carla,
to Andy, Mike, and Mark,
to JV, Ross, and Allison,
to Bryan and Jenna,
our precious grandchildren,
who make every day a HOLIDAY *for us*
when they enter our HOME.

And in loving memory of our son, John,
and our grandchildren, Kevin and Jeffrey,
who are in their eternal HOME.

Contents

3—Giving Thanks

4—Traditions

5—The Power of Example

6—Consider Yourself at Home

Preface

This book is a partnership among Habitat homeowners and well-known people from all over our country. Partnership is the essence of the Habitat program of providing for God's people in need.

A lot of fortunate people like me, who have never really suffered, get to know people like my friend Annie Mae Rhodes. It opens a channel of communications, friendship, love, and understanding.

Habitat for Humanity builds a lot of houses, and that's what people talk about. But the partnership among people of various backgrounds is a unique and beautiful opportunity for the homeowners and volunteers.

Jimmy Carter
Former President of the United States
Volunteer, Habitat for Humanity

Introduction

It never ceases to amaze me when I see what can be accomplished when people of faith and love go to work together. In 1992, the dedicated people of Atlanta Habitat for Humanity went to work and published a collection of mementos from one hundred prominent Georgians. The proceeds from that book, *A Christmas Housewarming*, made it possible for four families to escape poverty housing by building and buying their own Habitat homes.

The very first house built with book proceeds was unique. Margaret Quinlin, president of Peachtree Publishers, some of her staff, and Carmen Agra Deedy, author and contributor to the book, all worked alongside the new homeowner family to help them build their house. I wish I had a picture to show you of Margaret and Carmen wielding their long-handled shovels, up to their ankles in mud! It was an exciting day, full of joy, love, and just plain fun.

Now we have put together a collection of stories from prominent people from all over the country, so that we can build homes for many more families, and in all fifty states. Habitat now exists in over 1,100 towns and cities and in over seven hundred locations in forty-three other countries.

A few months ago I was visiting Habitat

affiliates in Oregon and Washington and speaking at various events. While there, I learned about Charlie. He is a little boy whose family was chosen to have a new Habitat house. When their family was told that they were getting a new house, Charlie started jumping up and down, yelling, "We won! We won! We won!"

The house was built over a period of several weeks. Then the happy family moved in. Soon, Charlie's grades in school improved tremendously.

Did the new house have anything to do with that? Did the fact that he had a room and a place to study have anything to do with his better performance in school? What do you think?

On behalf of the families who will benefit from this publication, thank you for your contribution in purchasing it. God bless you for being a partner in this ministry of hammering out faith, hope, and love. And, thank you most of all for helping more little boys, little girls, and their families "win"!

May your holidays be filled with peace and joy, and may they be enriched by the warm and wonderful stories in this book.

Millard Fuller
Founder and President,
Habitat for Humanity International

1

There's no place like home

Linda Mitchell

Human history is filled with the search for room to live, room to learn, and room to love. In Christian lore the most poignant search is the search of Mary and Joseph to find a place to bring their baby and our baby into the world. That they found finally only a cattle barn makes all human beings who hear the story one with the little baby born in the manger.

We are at our best, we human beings, when we endeavor to make room for someone to live in peace and in joy. Habitat for Humanity is about the business and the beauty of finding and making room for those who have no space. I am proud of all those who participate in that ancient and new endeavor.

Maya Angelou
Writer and Scholar

On our arrival in 1963 the pewter skies of Decatur, Georgia gripped my Cuban father's heart with an unshakable frost and he fell into a terrible depression. With our exile in North America came the chilling realization that he had exchanged the balmy breezes of our Caribbean island for windows that had to be taped with plastic to keep out the abysmal winter winds.

On one particularly cold and wretched morning he told his one friend at the steel mill, Big Dee, of his longing for that island in the Antilles.

"Big Dee, this country is *el lugar de los muertos,* the place of the dead."

"What you mean, Carlos?"

My father cocked his head toward the steamy factory windows.

"I mean look outside, Big Dee—the trees they are dead, the grass she is dead—*el lugar de los muertos!"*

Big Dee laughed. "Carlos, it's winter. Ain't they got winter down in that Habana of yours? Them trees ain't dead. They sleepin'. Wait 'till spring come. Why you ain't seen nothin' 'till you seen a Georgia spring—dogwoods and azaleas, wisterias and forsythias..."

"For-what?"

"Forsythia. It's a flower. They're all flowers, Carlos. South is full of them in the spring."

Papi had been staring quietly out of the windows when he turned to face his friend. "In Cuba we had flowers in December."

Perhaps it was the mountains of unspoken loss behind those simple words that inspired Big Dee. Or it might have been something as human as one gardener's need to best another. But this old southern man harbored my father's words, and weeks later, on Christmas Eve, we received a knock on the door of our attic apartment on Feld Avenue.

A great hulk of a man in a faded corduroy jacket filled our doorway like an old grizzly bear. His hand held a single yellow rose, the stem carefully wrapped in aluminum foil. My father's hand shook to receive it.

Papi has always said he would not have survived that first terrible winter if it had not been for Big Dee. His was not only an offer of friendship, but a promise of spring.

Carmen Agra Deedy
Author and Storyteller

It's great to go home for Christmas. I learned this for myself early in my career as a congressman, but I was reminded of the importance of home recently, when I met two very special families.

In December of 1985 Congress worked nearly around the clock and adjourned for Christmas at four A.M. After the long drive home, we had only Christmas Eve to make plans for a family celebration in Georgia.

In spite of our fatigue, we wandered around town, bought one of the last trees available, and did all of our Christmas shopping for the family in the closing hours of the shopping season. That evening, we were exhausted but relieved as we stopped to put everything together.

On Christmas Day, we saw our families and rested after a busy autumn and hectic holiday preparations. Luckily, all the presents that we had bought at the last minute turned out to be the right ones. It was worth all the effort to spend a Christmas at home.

Two families I met recently—the Schmidts and the Williamses—reminded me that having a home was the best present they could have.

These two families spent Christmas 1994 in homes built by Habitat for Humanity. Habitat is a great program where people reach out to each other across racial and class barriers.

I look forward to Christmas each year, of course. In the future I will look forward to it not only for my own family, but also for those whom I can help—through Habitat for Humanity—to have a home of their own for Christmas.

Newt Gingrich
Speaker,
United States House of Representatives

Speaker Gingrich is an enthusiastic supporter of Habitat for Humanity. "Building With Newt" is an organization which raises funds and provides volunteers to build Habitat homes.

If I had to put into a single thought what I am most thankful for, it would be hard to find a place to start. But I think I would have to begin with the most important things in my life—family and good health. My family was drawn even closer together by a tragedy that took the life of my sister Jane. Now, during the holiday season, my family takes special note of the things that mean the most to us.

We spend as much of the holidays together as possible. I treasure this special time and stress to my daughter the importance of carrying on this tradition.

Even though my brothers and sisters all have their own extended families now and time is scarce, we look forward to laughing together, eating my Mom's great cooking, and remembering to thank God for all our blessings over the past year.

Dan Jansen
Olympic Gold Medalist,
Speed Skating

Julie Hagan Bloch

Christmas is always a special religious holiday in our Catholic family. I can remember one Christmas that was not only special, but also the most unusual.

This happened a while back, when I was in the process of working my way to the big leagues. I was a left-handed pitcher trying to earn a spot on the Brooklyn Dodgers.

My wife, our little baby girl, and I went to Cuba for the winter baseball season. It was our first Christmas away from home.

There we were, a young family, trying to start a career in baseball, when the Cuban revolution began. Talk about your distractions!

I guess these unusual circumstances combined to make that Christmas all the more special. It certainly is one holiday that my family will never forget.

Tommy Lasorda
Manager,
Los Angeles Dodgers

Jim Starr

Who would think that a phone call could bring so much joy? Just ten days before Christmas in 1988 Tom Chapel called me to tell me the junior high youth group from St. Luke's Church was giving a party for me and my family. It was to be at our new Habitat house. I argued over the phone that it must be a mistake, I didn't have a house. But it was true! I was to pick up the keys to my new home a few days later.

This was the year we all were out to help someone. My son Derek helped me deliver baskets to homes for the YMCA. My son Corey was in a play where all the money raised went to homeless children.

When someone asked, "What did you get for Christmas?" I could only say, "A NEW HOUSE!"

Thanks to God, Habitat, St. Luke's, and everyone who helped on the house.

Sharon Collins

Holidays are always the busiest time for performers—living up to their job description and performing, usually on the road, far away from home and loved ones.

That's why I consider my very best Christmas the *one* time I was able to spend at home together with my wife and five daughters. The hugging quotient reached its highest levels as dancing flames in the fireplace provided a rosy background glow to those six beautiful faces I was miraculously able to enjoy at this special time. It wasn't a makeup Christmas, requiring stretches of the imagination, but the real thing. No long phone calls from Brazil or Sri Lanka; the sound of the voices had only to carry a few inches or feet, not thousands of miles.

When you're used to being far away, you do not accept nearness as a casual thing. You can feel so keenly the privilege of enjoying something you simply cannot take for granted, not knowing how soon or how long it will be until it can happen again.

That Christmas really drove home the meaning of the saying, "Home is where the heart is!"

Paul Anka
Entertainer

The homeless men gathered outside the Salvation Army shelter, lining up in their traditional orderly fashion. These men could tell every imaginable story of misfortune. Some were alcoholics or drug abusers, but some were just mixed up folk who needed someone to offer them assistance.

As the men filed in, you could see the thanksgiving in their eyes for the facility—a fresh, clean, warm place—a sort of family they could call their own. After finishing a hearty meal, they settled into their bunks for the evening.

The doors were locked and everything seemed quiet when the staff heard a pounding at the main door. Hurrying to investigate, they discovered a badly beaten homeless man. They took him in immediately, washed him up, took care of his wounds, and settled back to listen to his story.

This homeless man lived under a bridge close to the shelter and had had an argument with some other homeless people who decided to take over his location. He worked for minimum wage at a neighboring commercial institution. His wages were so low that he could not afford a home or an apartment.

That evening, the Salvation Army found a place for this man and also invited him to be a participant in the new "Two Dollar Program." Reviving a custom from the old West, this program allowed the men to purchase a bunk and two hot meals for only two dollars a night, and even reserve a space a week ahead.

The Salvation Army started this program to allow homeless people to regain a feeling of pride and to accumulate the necessary dignity to surmount overwhelming problems. At present, up to three hundred men each night are crowding into this new homeless shelter with renewed hope. They are welcomed even if they are not able to pay the two dollars a night.

The Salvation Army continues to recognize and love the unloved and to seek them out from under bridges and warehouse docks in the legion of the lost, sharing their grief and despair. With their banners and bonnets, they bring help not only at Christmas and Thanksgiving but throughout the entire year.

Richard C. Tucker
President,
Tri-State Bank, Denver and Boulder

I'm thankful that Millard Fuller and Habitat for Humanity have raised the issue of habitat, housing, shelter for God's people in need all over the world as a basic human right that can be realized in our time.

If Habitat can do what it has done in just a few short years, then how much more can we do in the remainder of this century?

It is possible to make housing a human right that can be granted to all the citizens of the United States of America and to all the citizens of the entire planet.

Andrew Young
Chairman,
Atlanta Committee for
the Olympic Games,
Former Ambassador to the
United Nations

2

The gift of oneself

Leavenworth Jackson

I am indebted to many, many people. I am particularly indebted to those who have reached out to me, not only by praying for me, but also by being my friend; who knew often just the right moment to call or drop a note, to send a book, to let me know they were thinking about me.

I have received many gifts—wonderful gifts. But none have meant more to me than the intangible gifts—like the gift of Compassion.

This was given to me with the admonition, and warning, that I would be called upon to show compassion to endless lines of suffering ones.

And the prayer that came with the gift of compassion was that I would never try to rely on my own reserves, but to draw freely and regularly from the One whose storehouse is always full.

It is my very firm conviction that there is a growing awareness of the need for a spiritual renewal in our country, and a willingness on the part of many to act and work in good faith together to fill that sense of emptiness with an outreach that is grounded in real Christian values.

Hillary Rodham Clinton [19]

Hillary Rodham Clinton
First Lady of the United States

I looked out at my audience and saw many of my baseball friends from over the years. Moose Skowron, Hank Bauer, and Bobbie Richardson were all there from my 1961 team, maybe the best Yankee team I ever played on. Roger Maris had left us, but his son, Kevin, was there, looking so much like his dad, it was amazing. Bob Costas had flown in, as had Coach Mike Fratello and Roy Firestone. There were too many others to mention. But they had all come to the Harbor Club in Greene County, Georgia, to help us raise money. I told them that night, "One of the really nice things about being a so-called celebrity is that you can lend your name to do something for others who can't do for themselves."

It had been the idea of my agent, Greer Johnson. We had hosted golf tournaments before at the Harbor Club. In the second year, Greer decided that the Harbor Club residents should do something for the less fortunate of Greene County. In the fall of 1993 we put together our little golf tournament and we were able to get gifts and items of need for 750 families. I was pretty proud of that. But 1994 was even more special.

As I stood on the podium at the Harbor Club, I announced to my friends and all of the people attending our post-

Jim Starr

tournament function, that this had been the first time I had remained sober during an entire tournament. I could not believe how much work had gone into the tournament from all of the volunteers from the Harbor Club Owners, manager and staff, from the homeowners at Harbor Club, and especially from Greer. I had the good fortune to play on twelve Yankees teams that won American League Championships and on seven World Champion Teams. But as I looked out at my audience I told them all, "This was the best team I ever played on." I guess that brought a tear or two to everyone. I have to admit, as I thought about the children who might enjoy Christmas a bit more thanks to this tournament, I was a bit choked up myself.

We had hoped to raise $100,000 from the tournament. The proceeds were to be split between several charities, including the flood victims of South Georgia and the less fortunate children and families in Greene County, who might have had little or nothing for Christmas without this event. But we flew past our goal and raised $131,000. Some of the money was given to worthy local charities. A lump sum was designated for the Red Cross to aid flood victims of South Georgia. Then Greer took a large chunk of the proceeds and spent weeks shopping and negotiating for Christmas items. In 1993 we helped 750 needy families; in 1994 we were able to offer bags of Christmas goodies to more than 1,050 families. All the gifts were organized according to age and sex of family members.

I've always said I was a very lucky man. Twenty-five years after I pulled off my uniform, people seem to still remember me. It's really nice to be able to use the name of Mickey Mantle to give something back. A lot of children in 1994 had a little nicer Christmas because of that golf tournament. I wasn't always able to be there for my kids. So it feels great to have been able to add my name to a great team and to have some small part in sharing a little Christmas joy with the kids of Greene County, Georgia.

Mickey Mantle 23
New York Yankees Hall of Famer

Susan Nees

At Thanksgiving I am reminded to renew the dedication I made in 1968.

There is no way to adequately express my personal gratitude for the kind deeds, the thousands of tributes and memorials from around the world to my husband, except to dedicate my life totally to the fulfillment of his dream.

Coretta Scott King
Founder,
Martin Luther King, Jr., Center
for Nonviolent Social Change

The Blue Bowl

When I was a little boy, younger than my sister, only eight or nine, my father, mother, sister and I lived in the country outside Farmington, Indiana. This was in the forties.

Without lament or particular sadness or regret, I often wonder about what happened to, and why we had, certain family customs and traditions. I know that some of them would be an embarrassment to modern politically correct and multi-culturally sensitive people of our day.

The blue bowl sticks in my memory as one such custom, or tradition, if you will. It was my mother's bowl and it was for my father's use. It was brought out at Christmas dinner. There was always something special in the bowl for my father. It was usually lovely to see, aromatic, and presented with a flourish that was alien to my mother's manner. Something that was time consuming to prepare and for which the ingredients cost dearly to a poor farm family.

My sister and I would sit at the Christmas dinner table and watch without emotion or envy as my father enjoyed the special treat in the blue bowl. When the dinner was over, the blue bowl was washed and wiped shiny and placed back in the cupboard until the next Christmas.

When my father was absent my mother would explain the blue bowl. "A man's home is his castle," she would say. "It is right for him to be treated special. Your father works hard and worries harder to keep us warm and safe."

It was her way of doing something tangibly special for our father, and our understanding of it was the way my sister and I acquiesced to the custom.

My father died when I was fifteen and many of the farm chores fell to me. We cut back on the big crops and gave up farming as a livelihood, but there were still cows to be milked, chickens to be fed, and wood to be chopped. I don't remember it as terribly hard work. I should say here that I knew little or nothing about the economy of our situation in life. I don't remember caring or thinking about it.

My father did not die a spectacular death, if death can be anything less than spectacular. He got sick, died, and was buried in the family cemetery. As far as I was concerned, things went on at the farm the way they had before. My sister took a job as a clerk at a store in town. She walked back and forth to work. It was a distance of more than two miles. We were a happy family. With my schoolwork, farm chores, and evening

Cristine Mortensen

radio programs, life seemed to hum along with little trauma. I was a strong young man.

Before my father's death our toys had been homemade. He was good with tools and had a flair for making things from wood. He could make toy trucks on which the wheels would roll. He once made a crossbow for me. It was of such construction that I could hunt small game and spear fish with it. When the first Christmas after my father's death came, I wondered some about the gifts I might receive.

My sister came home the day before Christmas and carried a large bag of boxes and packages. It was exciting to behold them. We had seldom had such beautiful colors and ribbons under our little tree.

On Christmas morning I unwrapped a beautiful, big, red dictionary. I opened the pages and smelled the inside of the book and realized that it was all mine. I thanked my sister and my mother and retired to my room with my big new dictionary to listen to the news on the radio and to look up some strange wonderful words I would hear.

And then it was time for Christmas dinner. We had the usual special holiday fare: roasted chicken, dressing, and all the trimmings.

I got a hint of our new financial situation when my mother asked the blessing. She spoke of my sister's sacrifice of her education so that mine could continue. She spoke of hard times, now passed, that I had not really been aware of. She gave thanks for my sister's promotion to assistant manager of the store where she worked, and added that we were grateful for everything.

I had brought my new, big, heavy dictionary to the dinner table and was browsing through it when I heard a small clatter that caused me to look up. My sister was eating something that looked wonderful. She was eating from the blue bowl.

Tom T. Hall
Entertainer and Author

30

I receive a lot of letters from listeners asking me to play requests and dedications on my radio shows. Among the most memorable is the one I received from a ten-year-old girl, Chelsey, in Washington, D.C., who asked guests at her birthday party to bring canned food instead of presents. The next day, she and her friends took the food to a homeless shelter. She asked that we play "One Moment In Time" by Whitney Houston and dedicate it to the homeless and all those who work so hard to help them.

I was so taken with that idea that my wife, Jean, and I began asking guests to our daughter's birthdays to bring canned food for the homeless instead of gifts, and guests to our year-end holiday parties to bring used clothing. These, in turn, are donated to local homeless shelters.

In the past few years, we've collected several truckloads of clothing this way, and a considerable amount of canned food. All this because one person wrote a letter and expressed her wish to help others.

Casey Kasem
Radio and Television Personality

Shelley Lowell

On a cold Christmas Eve in the 1950s, having just completed a midnight broadcast with the NBC Symphony under Guido Cantelli, the Robert Shaw Chorale of thirty professional singers hurried by private automobiles to Riverdale just above Manhattan Island, where—by previous arrangement with Arturo Toscanini's son Walter they were to serenade the "Maestro" with their most recent recordings of carols.

Met at the door by Walter, who cautioned silence, we were surprised to be asked into the "grand salon." Arranging ourselves on the most impressive of marble staircases, we began to sing...and sang and sang.

The "Maestro" shuffled out from the adjacent library (where he had been watching wrestling on TV), tears rolling down his cheeks, insisting on more and more singing.

As we finished, doors were opened to a dining room table loaded with Italian pastries, cheeses and wines.

To each member of the group he said a personal and extended thanks throughout a Christmas Eve which lasted nearly to the break of day.

Robert Shaw
Music Director Emeritus,
Conductor Laureate
Atlanta Symphony Orchestra

Christmas has always been a time to give. Several years back I was asked to raise money for a hospital in Los Angeles to buy gifts for physically challenged children. So, I set up a chestnut stand and sold bags of warm chestnuts that we roasted right in front of one of those fancy Beverly Hills boutiques. I sang "Chestnuts Roasting on an Open Fire" for nine hours and sold bags of the warm fat-free nuts to Tony Curtis, Henry Winkler, and literally thousands of people who were just shopping.

You can imagine how many bags of chestnuts I had to sell so that hundreds of children could have something very special under their tree. I've always been considered a little "nutty," and a pretty good salesman—this combination made it a very memorable holiday season!

Richard Simmons
Fitness Guru

Ramune

"Outta my way," a purposeful young voice sounded out cheerfully from behind. I jumped to the side, juggling the stack of Styrofoam plates that I was carrying. A red and white blur dashed past me, calling out words of holiday cheer as he bulldozed his way from room to room. I leaned back against the wall and watched in amazement at his boundless energy because I knew that he'd been hard at work even before I had arrived.

I'm Jewish, but I celebrate Christmas in a special way each year by volunteering—along with approximately three hundred others—to serve food to the hungry, bedridden, and lonely folks of Atlanta. When I first heard about Hosea Williams' idea to feed thousands of the city's people on Christmas Day, I knew I had to be a part of it and since then I have spent many Christmas days in this manner. Many of the dinner guests are fed in a public school located in Atlanta's inner city, but those who are unable to get to this location can benefit instead from the delivery service.

One year I had the privilege of delivering full plates of the left-overs, including turkey, dressing, sweet potatoes, collard greens, desserts, and fresh biscuits to Antoin Graves, a high-rise apartment building for the elderly. We set up our headquarters in the lobby and dished out a couple hundred plates of food. Other members of our team went floor to floor, knocking on every door and greeting folks with a Christmas meal. Many of these people invited us inside their rooms to thank us and share parts of their lives with us. One elderly woman who had no family invited us in to see how she made hats. Another sweet little lady sat in her wheelchair singing her favorite Christmas carol as she wept with joy for our greeting.

But most memorable to me was the smiling, energetic ten-year-old boy who kept darting in and out of residents' rooms. I watched him for most of the afternoon, happily delivering food and volunteering for every job that needed doing. Most of the kids I know would have been upset in spending the holiday feeding elderly folks instead of sitting at home playing with all the toys that Santa had delivered. Intrigued, I finally cornered him in the hall on the fourth floor.

"Merry Christmas," I blurted out.

"Merry Christmas and good cheer to you," he responded. He was carrying a pile of about a dozen covered plates.

"Some way to spend your Christmas, huh?" I asked, hoping to engage him in conversation.

"This is the best Christmas I've ever had," he said with a big grin.

"What do you mean?" I questioned him. He was anxious to continue his deliveries, I could tell, so I didn't want to detain him for too long.

"Mom and Dad said I could have one wish for Christmas. I asked if we could come and feed the hungry." He glanced up quickly at the sound of approaching footsteps down the hall. His face lighted up with recognition. "Oops! Here come Mom and Dad with some more plates. I've got to deliver these pronto."

Later on, I approached the parents to talk to them about their son's wish. I asked them if it was true, that their son had elected to feed the hungry rather than open gifts Christmas morning. They nodded their heads with pride.

"I never would have believed it if I hadn't heard it with my own ears," the father said, grinning from ear to ear. "He didn't even want any presents this year."

The mother nodded, "All he wanted to do was cheer people up on Christmas Day and if that's not the Christmas spirit, I don't know what is."

I couldn't have agreed more.

Neil Shulman
Physician, Author, Stand-up Comedian

3

giving thanks

Stephanie Smith

A Thanksgiving Prayer

40 Our lives are gifts from God, given a
day at a time.
Only today is in my hands, to do with as
best I can.
Yesterday is gone, beyond reach and
beyond change.
I can only learn from it.
Tomorrow and all it holds is God's secret.
Even its coming is not sure.

Only today is mine.
God, help me to do with it what will
　　please You.
Let me do well enough that I can offer it
　　with pride and joy...
　　and deep Thanksgiving.
Lord God...we thank You for our freedom...
　　and pray You will yet let it flourish
　　in the world.
We thank You for our families and all
　　we love...
　　and pray You will ever hold them in
　　the hollow of Your hand.
We thank You for our health...
　　and pray You will give us the cour-
　　age to bear its failings.
We thank You for the deep joy of work...
　　and pray You will help us meet its
　　challenge.
We thank You above all, dear God, for
　　the Earth...
　　and all its bounties.
May we, your children
　　and all our seed, strive here to please
　　You.
Forever and ever.
Amen.

Charlton Heston
Actor

Thanksgiving is a time to be grateful for everyone around us.

There is a wonderful fable that tells of a young girl who is walking through a meadow when she sees a butterfly impaled upon a thorn. Very carefully she releases it and the butterfly starts to fly away.

Then it comes back and changes into a beautiful good fairy. "For your kindness," she tells the little girl, "I will grant you your fondest wish."

The little girl thinks for a moment and replies, "I want to be happy." The fairy leans toward her and whispers in her ear and then suddenly vanishes.

As the girl grew, no one in the land was more happy than she. Whenever anyone asked her for the secret of her happiness, she would only smile and say, "I listened to a good fairy."

As she grew quite old, the neighbors were afraid the fabulous secret might die with her. "Tell us, please," they begged, "tell us what the fairy said." The now lovely old lady simply smiled and said, "She told me that everyone, no matter how secure they seemed, had need of me!"

We all need each other.

Leo Buscaglia
Author and Lecturer

Homer L. Springer, Jr.

Mary Jones

I'm thankful for the noise birds and frogs make, for the sound of certain words and names like "cranberry," "jubilee," "refrigeration," "Boone," and "Bobby Lee"; for the slow movements of fire and wood together in a fireplace; and for the possibility of a hot coal being dropped into water or hot lava sliding into the ocean. I'm thankful for fried okra.

And I'm thankful that I've always had a good home and a good family.

Clyde Edgerton
Novelist

Leland Burke

Thanksgiving is a time to remember our many blessings.

When I think of the many blessings in my life, I'm especially thankful for the relationships I have enjoyed with my family and friends.

46

However, I am most grateful to Jesus Christ, who died upon the cross.

And to a mother who loves me.

Evander Holyfield

Evander Holyfield
Heavyweight Boxing
Champion of the World,
1990-1992, 1993

Our most memorable Christmas began in the Year of Our Lord 1976 when Millard Fuller started Habitat for Humanity.

Christmas 1988 brought a new belief in ourselves. It was a wonderful feeling when we moved into our new Habitat house with our two daughters and two sons.

We had lived in a run-down place before. Now we had new FAUCETS—everything—NEW. It was a new beginning for the Whitehead family.

We could relate to each other better. We celebrated the birthdays of new grandchildren. We celebrated the ownership of a home for our family.

And most of all we have a Christmas view of knowing that Jesus can bless, and that his blessings, through many volunteers, have helped us to write some of the memorable moments of the holidays.

47

Calvin and Ossia Whitehead

My parents were both educators. So it's no accident that I grew up with a healthy respect for education.

At Thanksgiving I remember how thankful I am for my parents' emphasis on academics.

I'm also thankful for Morehouse College. Because Morehouse focused on academics, I learned mental discipline. I majored in physics and then discovered engineering.

Off campus I continued my lifelong interest in track and field. But I had no coach—and no track! So I trained on tracks nearby, sometimes climbing fences to get in. Hurdles were the most difficult challenge for me, so hurdles soon became my chosen event.

That's where the physics and engineering came in handy. The biomechanics of movement and of weight distribution—all of the knowledge I had acquired during my studies—helped me improve my style and technique with the hurdles. My education helped me in ways I could never have predicted.

Linda Mitchell

Thanks, Mom and Dad. And thanks, Morehouse. You gave me the ability to do what I had to do.

Edwin C. Moses
Olympic Gold Medalist,
Track and Field

David Doyle

A Wish List for Wildlife

Perhaps because I am a zoo director, I find that the marvels of nature are always a part of my list of reasons to be thankful. Without the wonderful diversity of nature, our lives would not be as rich.

Someone once asked me what gifts I would put under the Christmas tree if I could give anything to the wildlife that means so much to me. If it were in my power to give whatever I wanted, I would give the animals a world in which they would enjoy the following gifts:

Appreciation for all the beauty they provide us and for the interest they have brought into our lives;

Empathy for their tremendous, ongoing life struggle;

Respect as equal life forms that share this planet;

Understanding of their lives and the vital role they play in ours;

Protection from exploitation on an international level; and

Space for homes that would be sufficient and never violated.

In return for these gifts, we would receive an even greater blessing—a better world to live in not only for us but for future generations. Nature would repay us with a balanced, healthy environment whose long-term benefits would outlive our short-term needs.

In this holiday season, I wish you a true appreciation for the marvels of nature and a deep desire to help us all choose the right road towards preservation and conservation.

Edward J. Maruska
Executive Director,
Cincinnati Zoo and Botanical Garden

At Thanksgiving and throughout the year, I am thankful for my God and my family. I grew up in Brooklyn, New York, one of five siblings. My father died when I was quite young, leaving my Irish Catholic mother to raise the bunch of us. She instilled the importance of faith in me, and my faith has comforted me all my days. In fact, family and faith keep me whole.

I will be grateful as well if I can show young people that they can succeed with patience and hard work. I want young people to arm themselves with knowledge, so that they can achieve their dreams.

Faith in God, family, knowledge. A formula for happiness. A formula for life.

Lenny Wilkens
Coach, the Atlanta Hawks;
Head Coach,
the 1996 Olympic Basketball Team

Scott B. Benjamin

Jim Starr

Thanksgiving is a favorite time for me. It's a time for family. And football is in the air.

My life has been my family, football players, and coaching.

What a great combination! And sometimes the football players are like family.

I try to help kids learn how to succeed. As long as I can do that, then I'm getting satisfaction out of the relationship.

Sometimes our locker room is filled with former Penn State football players who come to be with our squad. They're still part of the family. They want our squad to know that they have the backing of their former teammates. I almost get choked up. That's a moving moment for me.

Thanks to all my family—at home and on the football field.

Joe Paterno
Head Football Coach,
Penn State University

I'm thankful for music!

From the time I was very young I've been moved by music. It's been a catalyst for celebration, for discovery, just everything.

I think when I'm singing songs or when I choose music, I want to experience that—I still want to be moved by the music itself.

So I include myself in the audience. I don't feel I'm separated from my audience in any way.

Amy Grant
Singer and Songwriter

Amy Grant is a strong personal supporter of Habitat for Humanity, and the spokesperson for Target Stores, which also supports Habitat. Proceeds from Ms. Grant's 1995 American concert tour benefited Habitat for Humanity—ticket sales in each town went to benefit that individual community.

As I reflect on the many blessings God has given me, I am particularly grateful for the two most important people in my life, my mother and my wife, Gail. My mother raised my sister, my brother, and me by herself after becoming a widow in her early thirties. She dedicated her life to her children. Through her on-the-spot teaching and her unselfish example, she instilled in us strong Biblical values. Her abiding love and devotion gave us the self-confidence to be the people God intended us to be.

Gail, with her unconditional love, has provided the foundation for our marriage. We will celebrate our twentieth anniversary this year. We have had many exciting chapters in our relationship and each unfolding new chapter gets better. My admiration for her grows with every new year as she shows me new ways to define love. Our four children are a real blessing that we enjoy together.

Steve Reinemund
President and CEO,
Frito-Lay, Inc.

Thanksgiving is a time to reflect on your blessings. I consider my father to be one of the most important and influential people in my life, and I wrote this poem to remind myself and my Dad how grateful I am for him and for the things he has taught me.

DAD

When I was little, you showed me the
    way
And made me what I am today.
For all your guidance, caring and love
I thank my lucky stars above.
I caused you problems, worries, and woe,
For that I'm sorry, I hope you know.
You taught me how to stand on my own,
If only then, I wish I'd known.
There were times when I was mad at you,
For the little things you made me do.
But you were always there for me,
You let me be what I wanted to be.
I love you more than words can say,
And learn new things from you each day.

Kimberly Aiken
Miss America 1994

Christmas is a holiday that I've always viewed with a certain amount of dread. Not because I don't like it, but because each year it seems to creep up on me faster than before, as if to scold me for all the things I haven't managed to get done on time: the presents to buy and wrap for my wife, my children, my eight grandchildren and great-grandchild, the many functions that I must attend and the sheer frustration at not being able to be in more than one place at a time. Thus, I have always sneered at Christmas and grumbled at the many demands it makes on me.

I usually maintain this demeanor up until the day itself and then something magical happens, almost on cue. After a satisfying dinner with my family, I pull out a cigar, torch it, take a few puffs, and the secret of Christmas is instantly revealed to me in a cloud of fragrant cigar smoke. Gasping from the fumes, the women in our family curl their lips in disgust because they know a male-bonding ritual is about to ensue.

My sons join me in lighting up, and with the aid of our stogies we contemplate the mysteries of life, politics, business, sports, and all the other things men are so good at discussing but not solving. Each year we're convinced that our conversations are extremely profound—in spite of the fact that we seldom recall them the following year. But that isn't the point. Our purpose is to come together as a family and bear witness to our shared experience. Sitting there holding my cigar surrounded by those closest to me, I realize that Christmas is a time of gratitude for all-too-rare moments like these. Maybe I won't complain about it as much next year....

Harry Morgan
Actor

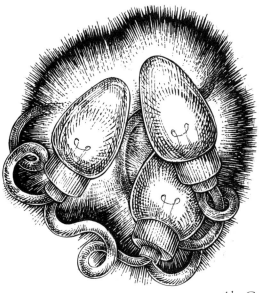

Abe Gurvin

I'm thankful for the influence my mother and father had on my life.

My father worked for a construction company and he was transferred every year or two, depending on where the work was located.

The first thing my family did when we moved was join the local church. The second was to go to the library and get library cards.

My mother did not believe in television. I grew up reading books, and I'm sure that inspired me to be a writer.

My father's family is a family of storytellers, and there were long dinners and lots of stories. As children, we absorbed them.

One of these days my writing career will be over. We've always said that we hoped we would look back and say we kept our feet on the ground, we didn't change, and it's time to go on to something else.

John Grisham
Novelist

4

Traditions

December 1, 1981: I was invited to put the star on top of the national Christmas tree on the Ellipse in front of the White House.

I went up in a cherry picker with a dear man named Joe Riley, who was and still is the chairman of the Annual Pageant of Peace.

This ceremony is not to be confused with the annual lighting of the Christmas tree. The tree is the same, but the events are two weeks apart. The President has the honor of doing the latter.

For the eight years George was vice president and the four he was president, up I went in that cherry picker. It was a wonderful, fun event.

Over the years, Joe and I took many of the grandchildren—Jenna and Barbara, Sam and Ellie, Walker and Marshall, Lauren and Pierce—and several schoolchildren to help us.

Some years were bumpy and some smooth; we went rain or shine.

Sometimes I felt a little like Mary Poppins.

Barbara Bush
Former First Lady, Author

Cristine Mortensen

Some years ago a fellow by the name of Elbert Jean moved in here from another state. Said he had been a Methodist preacher but had left the Church to enter the ministry. He wasn't exactly what you would call different; just didn't do things like most other folks. I discovered that he could make a ritual out of the most ordinary things. Like felling a Christmas tree.

Once he, two fine pointers, and I had driven from middle Tennessee to south Mississippi to hunt quail. More precisely, he had driven down; neither the dogs nor I did any driving. And the hunting part was a cover. It was almost Christmas and he pretended that he wanted to go hunting in Mississippi so he could take me to see my parents without acknowledging that he was a generous fellow and wanted to do something nice for a neighbor.

On the second afternoon, with no birds killed or seen, he said, "Well, here's a nice cedar tree. I think I'll take it back to Tennessee and dress it up."

I started to the house to fetch an ax and before I was out of sight I was startled by the BOOM! of his twelve gauge shotgun. I turned in time to see him shoulder a ten-foot tree and head for his car. He had felled the tree with one blast.

Late that night, driving up the

Natchez Trace, we were stopped by two young park rangers who accused us of having stolen the tree from Natchez Trace National Park property. Their uniforms, holstered weapons, and federal badges convinced me that we were in deep trouble. They said that unless we could produce a tag proving that the tree had been legally come by, they would have to give us a citation and impound the car. It was very dark and I was very scared.

Even with two bird dogs yelping in the back seat I knew it would be difficult to convince the rangers that what was tied on top of the car was really the prey of a two-day hunt, that it had been shot down on my father's farm, and that yeoman farmers in Amite County, Mississippi, didn't issue official tags when a son and his friend left with a cedar tree. But Brother Jean made shooting down a Christmas tree sound routine. Even appropriate and ceremonial. So they let us go. He did not tell them that the farm in Tennessee where I lived was a veritable cedar thicket.

Ever since, along about the middle of December, Elbert Jean shows up from Arkansas, east Tennessee, Kentucky—wherever he's living at the time—to shoot a Christmas tree. Over the years the ritual has attracted a sizable following.

Louise Britton

Neighbors began asking, "When is that fellow coming to shoot his Christmas tree?" They gather to witness what Pebo Cross from across the hollow calls "A tree assassination."

Waylon Jennings heard about it and brought his wife and son to see this strangely sacred act. A film maker from Chicago was on location nearby and followed with camera rolling to prove to Cook County skeptics that he had for sure seen a man shoot a Christmas tree and there was something tolerably reverent about it. Tom T. Hall was here on two occasions, not quite convinced the first time I suppose. A just defeated North Carolina congressman found a rung of healing in seeing that victory can be seen in defeat. All sorts of people, learning all kinds of lessons I reckon. Brother Jean says there is a ministry everywhere.

Through the years no one has ever asked Elbert Jean about his position on gun control. But don't go passing judgment on a fellow who shoots a tree at Christmas time. Leastways, not until you consider what will be on your Christmas table.

Will D. Campbell
Author

"Grandma's finest hour is the parade of the boxes at Christmas."

"Is she still saving all those boxes every year?..."

"No sooner is the paper off the present than she is winding the ribbon around her fingers and smoothing the creases out of the wrapping paper. Then she stacks them like Russian dolls, takes them home to her closet, arranges them by size, and waits for all of us non-box savers to grovel."

"You should see her closet. If Tutankhamen's mother had a tomb, this would be it. You've never seen such a box glut in your life. One year I tried to borrow one of her boxes and she reminded me that I jammed an afghan in one the year before

68

Diane Borowski

and broke down the sides. I said, 'Mother, I'm begging,' and as she handed one off the shelf said, 'Tell me what time it is to be opened and I'll be there.'"

Erma Bombeck
Author and Humorist

There are a few Christmas traditions that our family enjoys: being at home together in Plains; trekking through our woods to find a Christmas tree that is just right and all joining in to decorate it; and of course, the usual good foods, which must always include the Plains Special Cheese Ring.

One of the nice features of working with Habitat is providing homes for others, so they can develop their own traditions.

PLAINS SPECIAL CHEESE RING

1 pound grated sharp
  cheddar cheese
1 cup mayonnaise
1 cup chopped nuts
1 small onion, grated
Black pepper to taste
Dash of cayenne

Mix; mold with hands into desired shape (I mold into a ring); place in refrigerator until chilled. To serve, fill center with strawberry preserves.

Rosalynn Carter

Rosalynn Carter
Former First Lady, Author

Sylvia Vega

Christmas is tradition!

First comes our traditional Christmas Eve supper—an unusual but tasty, filling, and easy-to-prepare meal of oyster stew, Waldorf salad and peppermint ice cream. Then there's the last-minute wrapping of surprises to be put under the tree. Finally, we gather in a circle in the living room to share one of our favorite Christmas traditions—the reading of *Let's Keep Christmas*. This sermon by Peter Marshall, a Presbyterian minister from Scotland known for his powerful prayers, helps us celebrate the true joy of Christmas.

Our family has faithfully read this sermon together every Christmas for many years, with only the readers changing. Each year Peter Marshall's words about the real meaning of Christmas lift us up and remind us that Christmas is not in the stores, but rather in our hearts—and that we must remain open to the spirit of Christmas every day of the year, not just on the twenty-fifth of December. The sermon closes with a promise that we try to keep every year:

> "So we will not 'spend' Christmas...
>   nor 'observe' Christmas.
> We will 'keep'Christmas—keep it
>   as it is...
> in all the loveliness of its ancient
>   traditions."

Every year we are comforted and inspired anew by Peter Marshall's powerful reminder of what Christmas really is: God's promise and our hope.

John and Sue Wieland
Owners,
John Wieland Homes

 My wife and I hope that we will always be like children at Christmas, exulting in the scent of cinnamon and pumpkin, dazzled by the multi-colored lights on the tree, and allowing the sugar plum fairy to dance freely in our heads. But sometimes as the great day approaches, our sagging spirits need revitalizing and we retreat to a quiet corner to play our "Littlest Angel" tape—the one narrated by Loretta Young—and remember with nostalgia and bittersweet joy our children's many Christmases in our various homes in New Jersey, Connecticut, and Atlanta.

Christmas in the Boyce household may have been a bit simpler and more stylized than is the custom today, probably because my wife and I are more structured beings, but judging from the children's tender, and I hope honest, recollections, they were the stuff of memories.

72

Until all of our children were old enough for midnight mass, Betty and I divided our forces—one of us went to church at midnight, while the other crept out with the older ones to the earliest available morning mass. I can't believe the go-to-mass-in-the-morning spouse actually shepherded three or four tremblingly anticipatory children down the stairs and out to the car WITHOUT A

PEEK AT THE TREE! But the real accomplishment was actually sitting the whole brood down to breakfast after mass while the gifts remained untouched. Then, to take the whole choreographed ritual a step further, the long-suffering kids had to wait until I had the big, old-fashioned, cumbersome lights just right for the obligatory and usually dreadful home movies.

Homer L. Springer, Jr.

But at that point the dam broke, and all restraint was abandoned. The gifts from Santa, flashy, noisy, and hearteningly appreciated, were exclaimed over. New cars for the HO train set! A Daisy rifle! An Erector set! A puppet theater! And at long last, for the long-awaited girl, a beautiful lifelike baby doll complete with bottle and layette. Within an hour the floor was strewn with wrappings, our daughter had abandoned the doll for a fire truck, and voices had subdued to contented sighs of gratification.

Fortified with our second cups of coffee and grateful that we had once more brought together a day that was spiritually uplifting and naughtily materialistic, we would watch the wonderfully mobile and beautiful faces of our children (for all young children are inherently beautiful) and try not to imagine the vicissitudes that they and we would one day face, content in the knowledge that this splendid day, this priceless hour was ours to hold and love and cherish forever.

Ernest F. Boyce
Retired Chairman of the Board and CEO,
Colonial Stores Inc.

Holidays for me have always been a time for caring and sharing. I make it a point to celebrate them with people of different faiths so that we can learn from each other's heritages and experiences. Each religion, although different, shares a common denominator—love. All religions intrigue me and I especially enjoy being able to share my beliefs with others.

During the holidays I also make sure to include people who have no families, who live far from their loved ones, or who are estranged from their relatives. Holidays are a time to reflect on how fortunate we are and to show the special people in our lives how much we care.

Lillian Vernon
President,
Lillian Vernon Corporation

My wife, Mary, and I had the privilege of many a Christmas Eve gift exchange with our respective families throughout our childhood and teenage years. Our parents and other close relatives catered to each of us.

Later, in our early twenties, Mary and I established our household. We became the hosts to bring both families together for Christmas Eve.

We mixed our traditions and standards into a pleasing, new tradition. But we wanted to create some special element that would make our holidays memorable.

We hit upon the simple proposition of gifts to others. As we scanned the horizon for causes that were good and simple and affordable, we learned that C.A.R.E. and C.A.R.E. packages were looked upon with respect. We bought ten dollar C.A.R.E. packages for each member of the family, dressed up the certificates in a decorative form, hung them from our Christmas tree and had each of our guests in the course of the evening go to the tree and take their "ornament" from the tree. The total charity manifest in this modest action was hardly notable, but the spirit of the matter sparked each soul.

It turned out to be more than a symbol of a season of giving. The focus on others became a continuing tradition

Sylvia Vega

while we were the hosts for Christmas.

These acts of philanthropy bound our two families together for years to come.

Robert W. Galvin
Chairman of the Executive Committee,
Motorola Inc.

We would like to share with you a family tradition—our favorite Christmas dinner...

Quail in Gravy

In an iron skillet, melt 1/2 cup real butter. No substitutes.

Add 4 tablespoons flour and brown well.

Add 2 cups hot tap water and stir mixture until smooth.

Add to mixture 2 tablespoons Worcestershire sauce and 2 tablespoons lemon juice; stir.

Add cleaned, washed quail which has been salted and peppered to taste.

Cover and cook until tender in 325° oven, about 2 hours, basting often.

If thicker gravy is desired, remove quail from sauce, and thicken gravy with flour. Return quail to sauce for serving.

Serve with rice or grits.

Billy Payne
President and Chief Executive Officer,
Atlanta Committee for the
Olympic Games

Peter Spacek

When I was a trainee at the *Hollywood Citizen News* in 1951, my desk was right next to the city editor. One day she was reading a story about the Fresno Raisin Festival. She knew we were both raisin "nuts," so she called me over and showed me the winning recipe in the Fresno Raisin Festival Baking Contest—Pear and Raisin Pie.

It looked wonderful, so I took the recipe home and we fixed it for Thanksgiving dinner. It was so good that we've fixed it for Thanksgiving ever since. It's the greatest holiday pie recipe of all time.

Some fifteen or twenty years later, we had the whole family in for Thanksgiving dinner and of course we had Pear and Raisin Pie. But this version was a little different—my wife had accidentally used salt instead of sugar. But my son still wolfed down two pieces. It was so good, he never noticed.

Edwin L. Artzt
Retired Chairman and CEO,
The Procter & Gamble Company

Pear and Raisin Pie

1 cup water
½ cup juice from pears
1 tablespoon lemon juice
2 tablespoons orange juice
2 cups raisins
4 tablespoons cornstarch
1 cup sugar
1 teaspoon butter
1 cup diced pears

Heat water, pear juice, lemon juice, and orange juice to boiling. Add raisins. Boil 5 minutes.

Mix cornstarch and sugar together. Cook until clear and thickened. Add to raisin mixture. Add butter. Fold in pears. Let cool.

Pour into pie crust. Cover with top crust. Brush with cream. Bake at 450° for 15 minutes, then at 350° for 25 minutes.

Carole Boyce

As an only child growing up in a small apartment in New York City with my parents and grandmother, I always wished my family would one day celebrate Christmas in a house of our very own.

This wish never came true.

Nevertheless, this never stopped my father from enjoying Christmas and bringing the holiday spirit to others. For many years, I enjoyed watching my father dress up as Santa on Christmas Eve and deliver gifts to the children of our friends in the neighborhood. It was a special moment for me when my father asked me to join him for the first time.

When my father passed away in 1969, I was twenty years old, heartbroken, and unsure about carrying on his tradition. Surprisingly, the Santa suit fit better than I thought it would, even though it was a little loose in the chest. On Christmas Eve I squeezed myself into my '64 Oldsmobile with a bag overflowing with sports items, stuffed animals, dolls, and toy soldiers. It took me nearly seven hours to visit eight different families.

One family in particular stood out that night. The Joyners had six kids and I'll never forget the look on their faces. Later that evening I was told by a friend that my gifts to the Joyner children were the only ones they received that year because of the hard times the family was going through. After hearing this news, my chest swelled with pride and I realized that my father's Santa suit was a perfect fit after all.

And now twenty-five years later, my company, America's Favorite Chicken Company (AFC), is bringing the Christmas spirit to hundreds of people throughout the world. Energized by a five-year commitment to Habitat for Humanity, AFC will build homes for two

Betsy Kools

hundred families who have always dreamed of owning their own home— just as my family did.

Lisa Jones and her two sons, Rodney and Vanion, in Atlanta, Georgia, were the first family to share in this dream. This past Christmas, my sons and I joined some AFC employees to help Lisa decorate her new home for Christmas. The love in Lisa's home shone as bright as any reindeer nose could ever shine. Watching my own sons, Greg and Michael, help Lisa's sons hang ornaments on their Christmas tree allowed me to see how the joy of giving to others has passed through three generations of my family.

I look forward to the day when one of my sons asks if he can try on the old Santa suit stashed away in my closet.

Frank Belatti
Chairman and CEO,
America's Favorite Chicken Company

America's Favorite Chicken (AFC) is the largest sponsor and the only international sponsor of Habitat for Humanity to date. AFC has incorporated Habitat for Humanity International into its advertising campaigns, and plans now stand for each restaurant chain owned by AFC to raise money to build one hundred houses with local Habitat for Humanity affiliates, as well as provide the volunteers to do the actual building.

It once occurred to me that my grandchildren had never seen a live turkey and that they believed all turkeys came dressed like the birds they saw in the refrigerated display cases! But I know better.

As a child, Thanksgiving morning was both sad and exciting. A large turkey had already been bought and was tied by its leg to a stake in the backyard. A galvanized washtub was placed over it with only its neck sticking out. Grandpa would have my brother or me sit on top of the tub and chop off its head with a hatchet. The dead bird would flap so hard for a few seconds that he would lift the tub off the ground.

I was always saddened by the event because I was sorry to see the turkey killed, but that feeling disappeared as we all sat down to Grandma's Thanksgiving dinner!

85

Moon Landrieu

Judge, Fourth Circuit Court of Appeal,
State of Lousiana;
Former Mayor of New Orleans

Cheryl Mendenhall

Of all the formal holidays we celebrate, Thanksgiving Day holds a special
spot in my heart. I respect the truth of
Thanksgiving. It has not been commer-
cialized to the point that we miss the
whole reason for the celebration. From
those in modest dwellings with simple
meals, to those in the largest mansions
with huge feasts, we all have many blessings

for which we can be thankful.

I am drawn to the simplicity of this special day. It is a time to be humble and thankful for each blessing we have. I enjoy sitting around the table with my loved ones. I am thankful for the long journey that has brought us together again and grateful that our love for one another has been sustained.

We so often are caught up in pursuing the things we do not have that we overlook our greatest gifts: our attitude and approach to life; the human spirit that propels us forward and picks us up when we are down; the miracle of bringing a small new person into the world and the awesome responsibility of nurturing that human being toward his or her fullest potential; and the greatest gift of all, which is forgiveness.

I wish Thanksgiving were a season instead of just one day.

Chandler B. Barton
President and CEO,
Coldwell Banker Corporation

Coldwell Banker made Habitat for Humanity International its official corporate philanthropic partner in 1993. Many of the company's offices throughout the country also participate in Habitat projects on the local level.

If you talk turkey, turkeys talk back. Turkeys are—how can I put it—not too bright. Ah, but they are numerous on the broad range around Cuero, Texas, and the community must celebrate what it has.

Every year, in the crisp fall days before Thanksgiving, Cuero celebrates turkeys. Well, what would you do if you had to make a big deal out of a dumb bird? First, you would import a phalanx of fiddlers to play ceaselessly the municipal anthem, "Turkey in the Straw."

MAN: On your mark...Get set...

Since turkeys were made to gobble,

88

Lydia J. Hess

not gallop, there is not exactly a thrill a minute in a turkey race, but you have to go with what you've got, remember, and Cuero's got turkeys. After an eternity there are winners, and turkey trophies, which self-conscious boys accept on behalf of their puzzled birds.

Then you would have a parade, which moves along a trifle uncertainly, because of the unpredictability of its leading participants, five thousand turkeys marching down Main Street.

It is difficult to describe how dumb turkeys really are. Suffice it to say that the organizers of the Cuero turkey trot dread rain on parade day, because of the tendency of turkeys to tilt their heads back to drink, and then to forget to tilt them forward again, thus drowning right there on Main Street. The sun shone this year and the parade went off with decorum, but they haven't always, as J. D. Bramlette remembers.

J.D. BRAMLETTE: In the old days they was really in a mess because the birds were not domesticated. They were just wild turkeys raised on the range, and they ate acorns that fell on the ground. They weren't fed like our turkeys today are.

KURALT: So they were a little wilder when they got to Main Street, I imagine.

BRAMLETTE: Very much so, because when they saw the crowds of people, they became excited, and over the tops of the building and up in the trees they went, and this was a three-day job, to put them back into the flock and get them down to Cudahay Packing Company, where we were going to take them to market.

The sobering fact is that if there were no Thanksgiving there might be no turkeys, and if there were no turkeys there might be no Cuero, Texas. So while we all give thanks on this holiday, Cuero gives most deep and heartfelt thanks that once a year the nation takes all these dumb birds off its hands.

Charles Kuralt
Commentator and Author

5

The power of
example

Jim Meyer

BLUE SPRUCE

The example of my father has been a *powerful and lasting influence throughout my life. I wrote of this in a diary entry during my first campaign for governor. The following excerpt is from the collection of entries published in 1984:*

Whenever I'm feeling down, I can't help but wonder what Poppa would have said if I had told him I was tired or—God forbid—that I was discouraged. If I think about how he dealt with hard circumstances, a thousand different pictures flash through my mind—he was so used to dealing with hard circumstances. When he and Momma were struggling to raise us, almost everything was hard.

But one scene in particular comes sharply into view.

After living for years in the rooms behind my father's tiny grocery store in the city, we had just moved into our own house for the first time; it had some land around it, even trees—one, in particular, was a great blue spruce that must have been forty feet high.

The neighborhood was hilly. Our house sat ten or fifteen feet above the road itself, and the blue spruce stood majestically like a sentinel at the corner of our property, where the street made a turn, bending around our property line.

Less than a week after we moved in there was a terrible storm. We came home from the store that night to find the great blue spruce pulled almost totally out of the ground and flung forward, its mighty nose bent in the asphalt of the street. My brother Frankie and I knew nothing about trees. We could climb poles all day; we were great at fire escapes; we could scale fences with barbed wire at the top—but we knew nothing about trees. When we saw our spruce, defeated, its cheek on the canvas, our hearts sank. But not Poppa's.

Maybe he was five feet six if his heels were not worn. Maybe he weighed 155 pounds if he had had a good meal. Maybe he could see a block away if his glasses were clean. But he was stronger than Frankie and me and Marie and Momma all together.

We stood in the street looking down at the tree. The rain was still falling. We waited a couple of minutes for him to figure things out and then he announced, "OK, we gonna push 'im up!"

"What are you talking about, Poppa? The roots are out of the ground!"

"Shut up, we gonna push 'im up, he's gonna grow again."

We didn't know what to say to him. You couldn't say no to him—not just because you were his son, but because he was so sure.

So we followed him into the house and got what rope there was, and we tied the rope around the tip of the tree that lay in the asphalt, and we stood up by the house, with me pulling on the rope and Frankie in the street in the rain, helping to push up the great blue spruce. In no time at all, we had it standing up straight again!

With the rain falling still, Poppa dug away at the place where the roots were, making a muddy hole wider and wider as the tree sank lower and lower toward security. Then we shoveled mud over the roots and moved boulders to the base of the tree to keep it in place. Poppa drove stakes in the ground, tied rope from the trunk to the stakes, and maybe two hours later looked at the spruce, the crippled spruce made straight by ropes, and said, "Don't worry, he's gonna grow again."

If you were to drive past the house today you would see the great, straight blue spruce, maybe sixty-five feet tall, pointing straight up to the heavens, pretending it never had its nose in the asphalt.

And that's how good things happen: Dreams. A little common sense. Perseverance. Courage. Not quitting. And a little help from your family...and your teachers.

Mario M. Cuomo
Former Governor of New York

At Christmas, I like the smell of apples.

That is what we were given every Christmas at Vanna Junior High School, during a special assembly of grades one through nine.

Apples wrapped in paper. Large. Red. Sweet. The odor growing thicker with the unwrapping. The sound of bite and crunch from someone bold enough, or hungry enough, to start eating before the handouts were completed.

Apples and oranges and raisins on the stem.

Candy sticks.

For the boys, a pocket comb.

For the girls, hair pins.

Little gifts that seemed too fine to own.

And then Santa Claus would bolt in, yo-ho-hoing in a loud, familiar voice, and the older children would giggle with guesses about the pillow-fat man under the cotton beard while the younger children would stare at him in gleeful awe.

I cannot think of Christmas and not remember those years, those special December days of celebration, and the fly-back of memory is both joyful and melancholy.

On those days—more than any other time—I began to learn the difference between the haves and the have-nots.

The gifts we received were the same, and the yo-ho-hoing, pillow-fat Santa Claus treated us all with kindness and equity, but we knew—all of us knew—that it was only a temporary thing: the haves would have more, and the have-nots would not.

And the have-nots handled it better than the haves.

The have-nots hugged their gifts protectively and cherished them. The haves knew something better was waiting.

The have-nots took their apples home, to show.

Diane Borowski

The haves ate noisily on their way back to classrooms.

And that is the clearest vision I have of Christmas. Apples and children. Haves and have-nots.

But I think it's okay. I think that's what the day was about when it all got started.

Terry Kay
Author

Thanksgiving is a good time to reflect on how grateful I am for what my parents taught me.

My mother, for example, was always referred to as Sister Boston at church. She was known for her strong conviction that we should treat each other with kindness and always try to help one another.

Even after she died in 1991 at the age of ninety-four, people who knew her would say, "Thank you, Sister Boston," whenever they saw someone treat another with kindness. As a result of this training, I try to remember to help others whenever I can.

At the Olympics in 1968, I was competing once again in the long jump. I held the world's record at the time.

The long jump is a two-day event. The first day is for qualifying, the second day is the finals. Each person gets three attempts to qualify.

Bob Beamon had fouled on his first two attempts. One more failure and he would not be in the finals. I had already qualified and had taken off my spikes. I sat with Bob and calmed him down. I told him that he didn't have to win the Olympics that day—all he had to do was qualify.

It worked! He qualified on his last attempt.

The next day, on his first attempt, he jumped 29 feet, 2½ inches! He broke my record, and set a new world record. Bob gave me a lot of credit for helping him qualify. Had he known my mother, he would have said, "Thank you, Sister Boston."

Ralph Boston
Olympic Gold Medalist,
Long Jump

Leland Burke

The house was old and it creaked. It seemed that with the coming of snow, the creaks got louder, like rifle shots in the night.

We tiptoed ever so gently, knowing the steps like the keys on that old piano. Each step seemed to moan; we did our best to descend quietly. It took forever, one by one, as we made our way to the first floor.

Today, a hundred years later, I would dearly love to say it was his fault. But honesty—and a lifetime of guilt—compels me to lay the blame for that Christmas morning raid squarely on my own shoulders.

We weren't that old at the time, seven and three, but I remember being clearly in charge, bold and quite the little soldier, leading his troop into the fire.

"What can it hurt?" I fully remember telling the kid, "Santa Claus came, that's for sure, so what's to stop us from seeing what he brought?"

I seem to remember him muttering in protest, but I would hear none of it. (He claims today that I actually dragged him down those steps, him fighting the entire way, but I definitely don't remember that at all.)

The house was awkwardly quiet, save the creaks. Surely they would hear us—their bedroom was directly above. But we managed the assault with immaculate silence, opening everything under that tree within minutes. The paper flew as one present after another was torn asunder. Lord, it was a wealth of fortune!

And as the two of us ripped greedily into the last of our treasure, the lights suddenly came on and two astonished grownups stood sleepily in the doorway. Our cries to "come see" were met with angry sobs. In the years to pass—and it came up from time to time, as you might have expected—we learned how they had both worked several jobs to scrimp and save and somehow make that Christmas the best for their children. And how, by avoiding the stairway creaks, we had denied them the joy of giving.

It was, needless to tell you, not the best of holidays. But we never forgot the lessons we learned that night—lessons about "the season" and "the reason."

Jim Huber
Sportscaster, CNN

Christmas 1994 was my forty-third Christmas as a priest. Each one in its own way has been memorable, but in many respects, that Christmas will always be special.

Just before Christmas I visited a wonderful couple—the Reverend Mr. and Mrs. Scott Willis—who a month earlier had lost their six children in a van accident. Never before have I witnessed such faith. The Willises were a real inspiration to me. Janet said that at first she intended not to put up the Christmas decorations. But then she thought: "How foolish. Christmas is the celebration of the Incarnation, and that is what life is all about."

On Christmas day I visited a sixteen-year-old girl who was dying of AIDS, which she contracted as a result of a blood transfusion. During this visit she asked me to pray not for herself but for others, including her father.

But the real highlight of the season occurred on December 30. On that day I flew to Philadelphia to meet with Steven Cook, a young man who a year earlier had accused me of sexual abuse, then later dropped the charges. Even before he dropped the charges, I had written asking if I could meet with him to pray with and for him, especially because he was suffering from AIDS. Somehow he never received my letter, but a year later I learned he was eager to see me. He apologized for the hurt he had caused me. I assured him that I had never harbored any ill feelings toward him and was able to help him achieve the peace of mind he needs as he prepares to meet the Lord. It was a powerful moment of reconciliation.

The Christmas of 1994 will forever be etched in my memory. It was a time of love, compassion, forgiveness, and healing that I will never forget.

Joseph Cardinal Bernardin
Archbishop of Chicago

When my daughter was four years old, I flew with her to Greensboro, North Carolina, to visit my parents for Christmas. At the time, my father was seriously ill, and we all knew this was going to be his last holiday.

We were booked on one of the Christmas rush flights that everyone wishes they could avoid. Naturally, the flight was overbooked, then delayed not just for boarding, but on the runway as well. By the end of the flight, that plane was full of Scrooges anxiously waiting to carry their packages, luggage, winter coats and crying kids off of the plane. And since I was anticipating a heart-wrenching holiday, I must admit that I was faring no better.

As people collected their belongings and moved up the aisle to get off the plane, I tried to get my daughter into her red-and-white checked snowsuit. While I struggled to put her arms and legs in the right sleeves, my daughter stood up on her chair and began a deep-voiced Santa impression. "HO-HO-HO! Merrrrry Christmas!" She repeated it enthusiastically to each and every grumpy passenger walking past us. And they responded, in turn, with amused smiles and weary chuckles.

"What a marvelous situation," I

thought to myself. "This little girl, oblivious to the tension in the air, completely unaware of my own growing frustration as I'm trying to get her body into this snowsuit, is sharing her Christmas cheer with anyone who will listen."

With a simple "HO-HO-HO! Merrrry Christmas!," the bright spirit of my daughter's happiness not only changed my entire outlook on what Christmas would mean that year, but truly seemed to elevate the dour mood of many passengers squeezing past us as well.

*J. Veronica Biggins
Consultant,
Heidrick & Struggles, Inc.*

Linda Mitchell

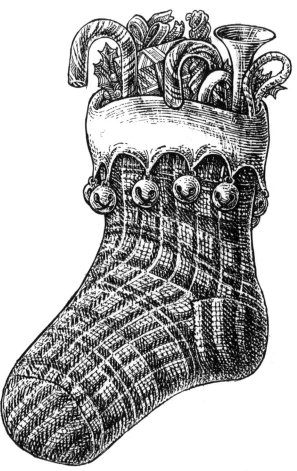

Abe Gurvin

The Christmas I remember most is also the first one I can remember. I was five years old and my mother, father, and I had just moved into a new house in Seneca, South Carolina. From the day the

Christmas tree arrived, my parents explained to me the meaning and spirit of Christmas.

My excitement rose as the presents began to pile up under the tree. As Christmas day drew closer, I was allowed to open one present each day. It took lots of inspecting and shaking and pondering for me to decide which gift to open!

Christmas morning I awoke at one A.M., charged into the living room, and began opening presents. My parents joined me briefly, then went back to bed. Later that morning when they joined me at the tree, I had opened not only all my presents, but all of theirs too! I was sound asleep in front of the fireplace when they found me, stuffed with all the candy that had filled the stockings hanging by the fireplace.

Each year when Christmas rolls around, I remember the impression that Christmas left on me. Even though the eagerness I felt as a child has lessened over the years, Christmas is still my favorite holiday.

Jimmy Orr
National Football League All-Pro,
Pittsburgh Steelers, Baltimore Colts

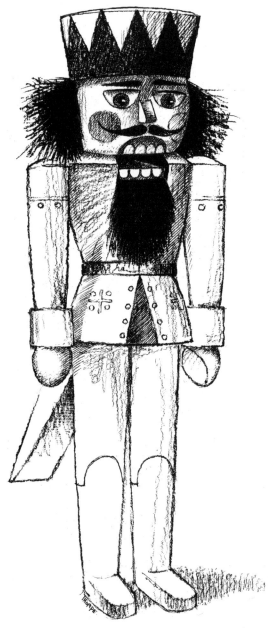

Jim L. Thorpe

When I think of Christmas, my mind takes me back to the Depression year of 1938. I was eight years old and our family lived in an apartment over a grocery store run by my Dad. We had a roof over our heads, good food, warm clothes and plenty of love. But we also knew many of our neighbors had almost nothing.

One of them was a boy about my age who lived with his eighty-two-year-old grandmother. They were very poor and, one day just before Christmas, he received a card inviting him to come to the Salvation Army headquarters in downtown Elkhart to pick up a gift. He asked me to go with him, and when we arrived at the old storefront headquarters, the Salvation Army officers gave my friend a present and laid out another present for me.

I was impressed by the generosity and deeply moved by the prayers and music. The sincerity was unmistakable and the sense of love was profound. But I knew I had a present under the tree at home. So when we headed back to our neighborhood, I left behind my gift from the Salvation Army.

When we got home, I told my Mom about the gift and she assured me that I had done the right thing. As

I was telling her how much I liked what I had seen and heard, someone knocked at the door. It was a Salvation Army officer and he was carrying the gift he thought I had forgotten.

Mom invited him in and explained what had happened. Later, I learned that she was a regular contributor to the Salvation Army. She was always helping people she knew, and by giving to the Salvation Army she was helping needy people she didn't know.

From then on, I followed her example. I didn't have many nickels and dimes in those days, but what I had, I shared with the Salvation Army.

So when Christmas comes, my heart smiles at the memory of those who taught me the lesson of sharing. It is a gift I treasure today and all the days of my life.

Arthur J. Decio
Chairman of the Board and CEO,
Skyline Corporation

My little six-year-old grand-daughter lives in a suburb of Charlotte, North Carolina.

Two weeks before Christmas she said to her mother, "I want to give Santa Claus something for Christmas."

"What do you want to give him?" her mother asked.

She came very near to her mother and said in a very faint voice, "I have to whisper it to you."

My little granddaughter has already learned the joy of giving—and she whispered her idea to her mother to make sure Santa's surprise would not be spoiled!

This child is being raised in a home where "the joy of giving" is taught by the good example of her young parents. She has already discovered this joy.

It is this same joy of giving, put into practice every day, that informs Habitat for Humanity's work.

George Beverly Shea
Soloist,
The Billy Graham Crusades

In a very real way most of us are trapped by the trappings of Christmas, no matter how we try to remember the shining *reason* for the Holy Day. We're trapped by not wanting to cause hurt feelings, by not being able to face one or more family members forced to be alone on December 25, by reckless overspending, by exhaustion from malls, and by long hours in the kitchen. But this is not going to be a suggestion for avoiding the entrapment, for "keeping Christ in Christmas." (How, in fact, does one keep Him out of it?) I am simply remembering one Christmas I spent *alone* under circumstances unusual enough so that no one was left out or hurt. My mother and father and only brother had gone to heaven, my best friend, Joyce Blackburn, with whom I share a home, was with her mother in Indiana, and I hied myself to Savannah, where, during the writing of the Savannah Quartet of novels, I felt most at home.

Christmas Eve and Christmas Day alone? Yes. Except for the One whose birthday we are supposed to be celebrating! He was *there.* Of course, I missed my family. Of course, I missed Joyce, but my conscience was clear and that Christmas some years ago turned out to be one I'll never, never forget. No one had to tell me to "keep Christ in Christmas" or to lighten up on the commerciality. My quiet hotel room held no presents to open, none to mail or wonder about—all that had been handled before I hopped in my car on December 23 for what lives still in my memory as the most deeply meaningful Christmas of my entire life.

Christmas in the South sounds artificial to Northerners who, like me, grew up hoping for white Christmases. But Christmas on St. Simons Island, where I live, can be, thanks to the glorious way in which God does His own decorating in our remaining stands of woods, not only warm enough to stroll outside, but a spectacle of sheer beauty. (And I'm not speaking of the usual garish display of colored lights in which Southerners indulge, too.) He decorates His woods with the reddest branches of holly and cassina berries and, wonder of wonders, He even leaves behind scarlet creeper and tupelo leaves on a few deciduous trees. To me, though, most breathtaking of all, He drapes any willing tree and bush and scrub oak with golden-leaved bullis grapevines, so that almost every growing tree is a veritable holiday treat! (One recent Christmas on St. Simons Island delighted kids and amazed adults with a few inches of snow which actually stayed on the ground and on the branches of dark green live oaks and cedars for well over a day. Even the palmettos and palm trees held the now odd-looking white stuff and actually looked a bit silly.)

I used to love white Christmases in my youth. I loved that one here in coastal Georgia, but glistening snow (and it does stay clean here) and colored electric lights and expensively wrapped gifts do not a real Christmas make.

I feel I experienced the true authenticity of Christmas, the Holy Day on which God gave us His greatest gift, on that one Christmas in Savannah spent alone with Him, whose Birth we celebrate. I experienced the unforgettable hours *inside* a peace uninterrupted by a single jangle or a single duty gift or greeting card. Those were all piled in my kitchen when finally I reluctantly abandoned the light of my blessed solitude and drove home.

The Light was still inside me, though, and the peace.

Eugenia Price
Novelist

Leroy Scott

It took me a long time to appreciate all the blessings I have received in life. But one day stands out as a turning point in my attitude.

Early one morning, the teacher asked each of us to bring two dollars to school the next day for supplies.

But then, without any embarrassing emphasis, he added that anyone who could not afford the two dollars could see him after class, and they could work something out together.

I remember being surprised that some people could not afford that amount of money.

On that day, when I learned to focus on others instead of just on myself, I began to grow up.

Steve Lundquist
Olympic Gold Medalist,
Swimming

When I recall my Christmas memories, I realize there is a common emotion running underneath. It seems that each holiday season leaves me with a deep-seated feeling of personal renewal.

At my company, fall is our busiest season. Since we make products specifically for home improvement and decorating, we all work at 150 percent capacity throughout the fall, getting ready for the start of "Spring Cleaning Season" come March. I love the work. I thrive on it. But business can be wearing. The travel can be particularly hard on your family, and sometimes you have to fight very hard against becoming cynical and discouraged.

116

Homer L. Springer, Jr.

That's why the Christmas season is so special to me. That time with my wife, Jackie, my daughter, Nancy, and her family, Tim, Austin, and Amber, renews my appreciation for the human values that can make a difference in a person's life. Seeing the season through the eyes of my grandchildren is particularly moving. They give unconditional warmth and acceptance. They laugh and express their joy freely. They enjoy the small gifts as much as the big ones (and sometimes more!).

And when I look at my youngest grandchild, Amber, my sense that life is a precious gift is renewed a thousand times. Health complications made Amber's birth in August very difficult and frightening for the whole family. Having her with us this Christmas is a special sign to remember what is truly important... to count your blessings and to share them with others. No matter what the previous year has been like, during the Christmas season my faith and hope are stronger, and I remind myself to do whatever I can to make others' lives better in the months to come.

Bill Stewart
President,
The Thompson's Company

Thompson & Formby, part of The Thompson's Company, promotes Habitat for Humanity nationally and provides waterproofing and paint products for its projects.

As we gather with our families to celebrate the Thanksgiving holiday, we are reminded of the origins of this celebration and the qualities of character exemplified by the early American settlers. One virtue intrinsic to their perspective that is just as important in today's world is responsibility.

Responsible persons are mature people who have taken charge of themselves and their conduct, who *own* their actions and *own up* to them—who *answer* for them.

We help foster a mature sense of responsibility in our children in the same way that we help cultivate their other desirable traits—by practice and by example.

William J. Bennett
Author;
Co-director, Empower America;
Former Secretary of Education

6

*consider
yourself at home*

When I was a small child, Christmas presents all seemed to be the same present, though, of course, they varied. From Santa Claus, a doll every year. One year she cried, another year she drank from a bottle and wet, one year she had "magic baby skin," one year she was an eternal bride-to-be, as frozen on the eve of her wedding as Keats' unravished bride of quietness. One year, when I was twelve, she was a truly exquisite Alice in Wonderland, a perfect, fragile, mini-woman. Later that day, goaded by God knows what mute rebellion, spoiled perversity, what rampaging new hormones, I shot her with a new Daisy air rifle. Dolls were gone from my Christmas Country after that, to be replaced by charm bracelets and pink angora sweaters and record albums, by the flimsy, useless, spangled Christmas things that I still love to receive.

There would be outfits. A nurse's outfit. A cowgirl outfit, complete with fringed vest, six-shooter, and miniature western boots. An appalling WAC outfit, for we seemed perpetually at war in that holiday country. Somewhere in my parents' house, small, grave me sights along the six-shooter into the camera still; lumpy, unlovely me salutes an unknown commander-in-chief under the patent-

Mary Jones

leather bill of a hideous flat-topped cap.

For my mother, a huge jar of blindingly purple bath salts that stank for days when she opened it. I had had my eye on it at Vickers' Five-and-Ten for half a year, and Mrs. Vickers had had to scrape the grime of unwantedness out of its mock cut-crystal when I purchased it.

My father would open the miniature hat box with the wonderful, perfect little hat in it, and a certificate that said he could receive the hat of his choice at an Atlanta hattery. Always, he said it was just exactly what he needed. Always, he bought the same hat.

Anne Rivers Siddons
Novelist

Mitzi Cartee

As the youngest of six children from a very close family, I always enjoy going home for the holidays to spend time with my mother and siblings. Hanging out in the warmth and familiarity of my mother's kitchen brings back fond memories.

We all sit around the table eating and telling stories, basically all talking at once and therefore making a lot of noise. It sometimes gets so loud that I get a headache before the end of the night. However, it is one of those comforting aches, much like the sore muscles I have after a really good workout.

Bonnie Blair
Olympic Gold Medalist,
Speed Skating

My mother is gone, but I still learn wonderful things about her. Such was the case on a Thanksgiving afternoon as our extended family sat around the table.

As the family discussion unfolded, I was into a bragging mode and was grandly telling everyone how independent and self-sufficient I was, even as a child. I reminded them that when I was seven years old, I declared my right to walk to school alone. Up to that point an older girl who lived next door to us in the heart of Philadelphia was paid twenty-five cents a week (big money in those days) to walk me to and from school. The trip was eight blocks and

Shelley Lowell

across many busy streets. My next door neighbor, Harriet, earned every penny of her pay, because I was not the easiest person to handle.

My mother didn't want me to go to school unattended, but through constant begging, she gave in to me. The agreement was that if I was careful, she would give *me* the twenty-five cents and not "waste" it on a neighbor.

My sisters, who are more than ten years older than I am, laughed when I told this story. One of them said, "Do you really think that you walked to school alone each day? If you did, you were wrong. Every day Mom followed you to school to make sure that you got there safely. And every day, she waited for you at the school door and followed you home again. She always hid herself because she wanted you to think that you were independent, but she was always there in case you needed her."

125

Tony Campolo
Professor of Sociology,
Eastern College

REINDEER <small>RAIN DEER (Cervus tarandus)</small>

THE REINDEER IS KEEN OF SIGHT, SWIFT OF FOOT AND CAN BE TAMED TO PULL A SLEIGH OVER THE SNOW AT A HIGH RATE OF SPEED... A SELECT FEW ARE CHOSEN FOR SPECIAL FLIGHT TRAINING BY SANTA'S ELVES.

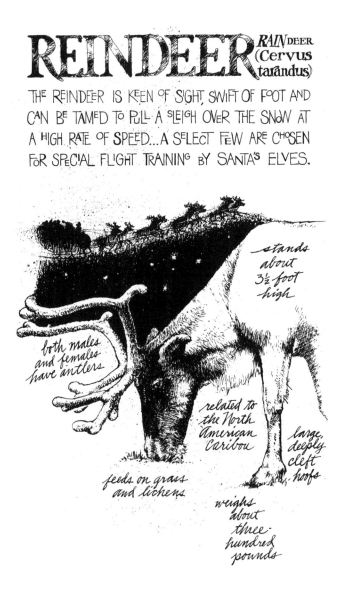

stands about 3½ foot high

both males and females have antlers

related to the North American Caribou

large, deeply cleft hoofs

feeds on grass and lichens

weighs about three-hundred pounds

Jim L. Thorpe

I grew up in New England, and remembering the holidays there always brings back memories of huge family gatherings.

The immediate "forty" of us would gather at my grandparents' home, where we would exchange presents, eat, and watch the snow fall silently on the evergreen and birch trees.

Being young and mischievous, my brother and I would often go under the dining room table during dinner, untie my uncle's shoe laces...then retie them to the folks sitting on either side of him. Of course, I would never get through this "mission" without breaking into laughter, ultimately blowing our cover.

At the end of the meal, my grandmother would lead us in the singing of "God Bless America."

Being in the news business, I rarely get home for the holidays. But I carry these memories vividly in my mind's eye so that no matter where I am, I can at least go home in my heart.

Susan c. Lichtman

Susan Lichtman
News Anchor,
Fox News, Los Angeles

I best remember Christmas as a time that reduced my brothers and me to a squirming bundle of barely contained joy, not unlike a litter of puppies. I also remember the endless schemes that we, as young boys, thought we were going to put over on old St. Nick.

One Christmas, my older brother, Kyle, and I decided that we would hide behind the Christmas tree in anticipation of the big boy in the red suit. Certain that our plan would net us a big fish, we sat giggling in excitement and, of course, began roughhousing in our tight little corner. The inevitable occurred barely minutes later when the tree crashed to the floor and two panicked boys flew from their hiding place. The next order of business was damage control. And who better to use for damage control than a little brother, who was appropriately named Noel. You can imagine our chagrin when neither Mom nor Dad bought our hastily contrived story. Certain that coal was in the offing, we were unceremoniously dispatched to bed much earlier than usual, while Noel sat basking in the glory of vindication, enjoying hot chocolate and freshly baked cookies.

The following Christmas, we were determined to not mess up. But somewhere along the line we came up with the idea of substituting Mom's freshly baked cookies, which were always left out for Santa, with the fruitcake that we knew was lurking beneath the tree, compliments of one of our smelly old aunts. Sniffing the packages as best we could when Mom and Dad weren't looking, we swiped the package that was surely the fruitcake, placed it upon the table where the cookies lay, and planted a scribbled note indicating that the treasure was all Santa's—enjoy! The cookies were messily devoured by four ravenous boys. The best-laid plans of mice and boys, however, were quickly discovered, which led to a ban on the living room on Christmas Eve to four very repentant brothers.

As an adult, I now see Christmas as a time to reflect on and give thanks for the birth of Christ. But with the addition of wriggling nephews and nieces, I am reminded that Christmas is always a time of wonderment—and almost uncontrollable energy—for children.

Gary Redenbacher
Marketing Spokesman,
Orville Redenbacher's Gourmet
Popping Corn

At the Kemp household, the holidays obviously revolve around two things—family and football. With three professional quarterbacks in one family, the challenge is getting everyone together under one roof on the day everyone else is celebrating.

With our backyard satellite dish, however, we usually can find the game in which one of those quarterbacks is playing, and bring him into our living room. That lets us share time together even if we can't spend time together.

Moreover, the wife and mother of those quarterbacks, Joanne Kemp, makes sure that not only our immediate family, but also the extended Kemp family, spend time together during the holiday season.

But most important, we also take time for our American family, particularly the least privileged, the lost, and those left behind. After all, as my mother always told us throughout the year, those of us who are blessed have an obligation to be a blessing to others.

Jack Kemp
Co-director, Empower America;
Former Secretary of Housing and
Urban Development

Christmas isn't just when you get toys and presents. It's very important to remember that Christmas is the birthday of Jesus Christ.

It's a time for giving. And the Habitat people gave so much, so that we could have a home.

I want to say thank you. And I hope all of you have a happy and jolly Christmas.

Marie Billings

Mitzee Cartee

Homer L. Springer, Jr.

The holidays always bring a flood of memories because they've been a source of great joy in my life.

One of my earliest recollections, as well as one of my fondest, took place when I was but five years old.

I remember that my parents and my sister and I lived in a duplex beside my grandparents and my great-grandfather.

I can still recall the feeling of love and caring that came from every corner of that duplex.

This particular event took place at Christmas. I had to learn the melody and memorize the lyrics to "Away in a Manger" and part of the Christmas story from the Bible to sing and recite in front of the entire congregation.

Fortunately, my entire family sat in the front row smiling and cheering me on. Though I was terrified and could feel myself getting hot and clammy, I vowed to do it all, and without a mistake. I wanted so much to make all of them proud of me.

I did it to the cheers of my family and the applause of the congregation. They inspired me to succeed in my "recital," and in my life. That was a wonderful evening, and it has stayed with me ever since.

Loni Anderson
Entertainer

The year that I became a senior officer with the National Association of Home Builders (NAHB), I persuaded my wife, MaryBeth, and our three children that we needed to build a new home.

The timing seemed perfect. With three active teenagers, we needed more space, and I knew that each year as I moved up the NAHB leadership ladder, the demands on my time would increase.

As they say, hindsight is twenty-twenty, and I quickly realized that the timing for this ambitious undertaking was not so perfect. Even during my freshman year as an NAHB officer, my schedule was full, and I was on the road and off the job for weeks at a time. As a result, our new home was nowhere near completion when Christmas came.

We had all been looking forward to spending our first Christmas together in our new home and were very disappointed when we realized that it just could not be. As an alternative, we decided to celebrate the season at our simple cabin on the Umpqua River, three hours from our home in Portland.

When we got to the cabin, we went straight to work to make it a Christmas to remember. We dug up a scrawny Douglas fir on our property and all five of us worked for hours making cookie

David R. Doyle

ornaments and decorating the tree with ropes of cranberries and popcorn. (Eager to participate in the festivities, our dogs helped make it a Christmas to remember by eating every one of our lovingly hand-crafted decorations later that night.)

Throughout the entire holiday, the little cabin hummed with the spirit of

Christmas and the entire family enjoyed a time of personal and spiritual renewal around the fireplace on Christmas Eve.

We realized as we shared this very private evening that home is where the family gathers, where the family grows, where the family gives to each other. It need not be elegant or fancy; it is where there is love.

Jim Irvine
President,
National Association of Home Builders

The National Asssociation of Home Builders, a federation of more than eight hundred state and local builders associations, partnered with Habitat for Humanity in 1992. The NAHB matched seventy-three local home builders associations with Habitat affiliates for the program "Homes Across America."

The Christmas and New Year season for me brings great joy—and travel miseries.

My daughter and her family live in Seattle, Washington, while my son and his family live in Gaithersburg, Maryland. The holiday frustration comes from traveling from my home in North Carolina to the Northwest or Gaithersburg in alternate years. But, regardless of the coast I'm on for the holiday season, I derive tremendous joy from the precious moments shared with my children's families, including three lovely grandchildren and one beautiful great-grandson.

An added joy of the holiday season is the opportunity to attend the Rose Bowl when I go to the West Coast, and the Orange Bowl or the Peach Bowl (sometimes both) when I'm on the East Coast. So no matter how much distance I must travel, I am truly grateful for the deep pleasures of the holiday season.

137

LeRoy T. Walker
President,
United States Olympic Committee

My fondest memories of childhood come from family Christmas trips to visit our extended family, the Donovan cousins. We were a family of five children from New York City to invade a family of eight children in the countryside of Brackney, Pennsylvania; when the weather was right, we spent most of our time outdoors.

The Donovan clan lived at the bottom of a rolling hill on a lake. What a winter wonderland! Sledding, tobogganing, ice skating, and skiing awaited us. The hill behind the house became a great sledding run. We would go up and down that great hill for hours and hours.

Skating was also great fun, but much harder for us city kids than for our country cousins. We would marvel at how well the cousins skated, especially when they donned the speed skates and proceeded to jump the many long docks jutting out into the frozen lake. Skating at night with the light from lanterns and flashlights was particularly thrilling; I can still see the shimmer of the light on the ice even now.

Brian Winters
Head Coach, Vancouver Grizzlies;
National Basketball Association All-Star,
Milwaukee Bucks

Ramune

The Dream House

It was the Christmas Eve of thirty years ago and all my children were still of the ages to be mystified by the secrets of Santa. I can't recall everything that was listed or wished for, but I do remember my oldest daughter's greatest hope was to have a Barbie Dream House beneath the tree on Christmas Day.

And Santa had one!

That night, when all my babies had gone to bed—to bed, not to sleep—I and my helpers crept about arranging what Santa had left behind. My "helpers" were my husband, Billy, and my father, William, who ritually got together on this night to toast the year past and welcome the one ahead. They toasted, and I took care of things.

The time came to set out my daughter's

Linda Mitchell

bounty. I opened the box and there it was, Barbie's Dream House in all its glory, majestically crafted of the finest pink and white plastic to be found. And in 96,000 tiny pieces. My helpers, still toasting, did the manly thing and volunteered their services. I was relieved and set about stuffing stockings and wrapping last minute gifts.

After an hour or so I went to check on the progress of the house and found my helpers with muddy shoes, empty glasses and *no* Barbie Dream House. "She'll never know," said Billy. My father agreed. "We can leave a note from Santa," he said.

It was explained to me that some pieces wouldn't fit the way they should and there was no choice but to dispose of Barbie's defective pink and white palace in a shallow grave behind the barn.

My daughter got a warm note from Santa with the promise of a house in the near future and my helpers got a stern lecture *and* a promise for the next Christmas. *No toys that must be assembled!*

Sybil Carter
Associate Director, Corporate Programs,
Habitat for Humanity, International

Leland Burke

Christmas is a time when we come together to celebrate the birth of Jesus Christ and the spirit of peace, and it is also a time of special closeness as a family.

After the 1972 Senate election, our family had to settle in Washington in the middle of the Christmas holidays. It was a memorable occasion for many reasons, but extremely hectic. Yet in the midst of uprooting our family from so many of its traditions, a new family tradition was born that Christmas.

Since we moved so quickly, all of our Christmas ornaments were still at our home in Perry. We decided then to make our Christmas ornaments by hand instead of buying new decorations.

Our children were ages three and six when they began creating their own decorations, and this continued through grade school. They painted plastic Santa Clauses and angels and put them in a hot oven to shrink. They decorated sea shells, sand dollars, pine cones, and the hulls from pecans and walnuts. They wove yarn around popsicle sticks; made cutouts from felt and construction paper; stuffed cut-out calico candy canes and Christmas trees with cotton batting; made shadow boxes out of egg shells; and constructed bird feeders from plastic pill cylinders and cardboard.

They learned that you can make any Christmas special with a little creativity and perhaps a little less commercialism. Each year we now enjoy a tree adorned with precious memories for all of us.

Sam and Colleen Nunn
United States Senator and his wife

ACKNOWLEDGMENTS

First of all, to all the generous people who contributed a memento or a piece of artwork to this collection, a grateful thanks is offered. You have lent your name and your time and your talent to help families escape poverty housing.

To the following friends who helped contact the authors and artists, I have a question, "Am I the luckiest guy in the world, or what?" The list includes: Jill Becker, Harris Bostic, Jane Bourdier, Beth Boyce, Betty Boyce, Anne Bridges, Connie Bryans, Sybil Carter, Paul Cropley, Chris Curle, Nancy Desmond, Allen Donaldson, Barbara Dooley, Bill Earnest, Susan Edmonds, Jane Emerson, JoAnn and Al Fluegeman, Newt Gingrich, Alex Hawkins, John Heald, Nancy Jackson, Ernie Johnson, Father Albert Jowdy, Elise Langan, Kathie Lesesne, Susan Lichtman, Mary Line, Sam Massell, Belinda Masters, Sam Nunn, Mary Ann and Tom Pacer, Rusty Paul, Frank Skinner, Donna Smythe, Bill Stelten, Gretchen and Jim Stelten, Betty Jane Trout, Tom Waters, John Wieland, Danielle Wilkshire, Julie Winters, Phyllis and Roland Wintzinger. I owe each of you a huge favor.

To Millard Fuller and Douglas Bright at Habitat headquarters in Americus, for your most valuable support. And a special thanks to Joy Highnote, for many hours spent contacting potential authors. It's a pleasure working with each of you.

To all the gang at Peachtree Publishers, and especially my talented and tactful editor, Stephanie Thomas, for your professional guidance and just plain hard work. And for your dedication to helping Habitat.

And to my dearest Jeannie, for your patience in listening to every crazy idea, your gentle persuasion, your loving support, and for being my best friend, and my wife. Thank you, my love.

Gene Stelten
Editor

Abe Gurvin

INDEX OF ARTISTS

Our special thanks to the following artists who generously donated their work:

call to Action

Habitat for Humanity International is a nonprofit, ecumenical Christian housing ministry that works in partnership with people everywhere to build simple, decent, houses with families in need. Habitat's goal is to eliminate poverty housing and homelessness from the earth.

Habitat affiliates in all fifty states and more than forty nations worldwide have built tens of thousands of houses that are sold to our partner families at no profit, with no interest charged on the mortgage. Partner family members invest hundreds of hours of their labor—sweat equity—building their houses and the houses of others. Habitat home ownership helps to break the cycle of poverty and brings new hope to families previously trapped in substandard, and often deplorable, living conditions.

You can be a part of this life-changing work! Join with the hundreds of thousands of Habitat volunteers around the world who have experienced the joy that comes from truly making a positive difference in the lives of families in need. Habitat welcomes your support through prayer, labor and financial gifts. For more information contact the Habitat for Humanity affiliate nearest you, or call 1-800-HABITAT, extension 551 or 552.

To make a tax-deductible donation to Habitat's work, please make your check payable to Habitat for Humanity International and mail it to:

Homer L. Springer, Jr.

Habitat for
      Humanity International
121 Habitat Street
Americus, Georgia 31709-3498